MW00973820

Diamond Del's
Search for the Crown Jewels

To my very own Diamond Del, Grace, and Rose.
Eph 6:10-18
-A.A.

Published by DDGMA, LLC.

Printed and Bound in the U.S.

ISBN 978-0-615-40010-5

www.diamonddelbook.com

Diamond Del's
Search for the Crown Jewels

By Anna Allen
Illustrated By Allen Sutton

To embark on a journey to foreign lands
And search for the greatest stones
known to man.

Diamond Del will travel around

To find the stones for a special crown.

A crown he'll place before the King.
A crown that only he can bring.

On true adventure he must embark

Deep into a forest cold and stark
To find Fluorite in midst of the dark.

Obstacles will always be in his way
So courage and honor he must display
To snatch the Tiger Eye away.

Danger and challenges he must address.
A spirit of peace he has to possess

To hold the Rose Quartz with great success.

But knowledge and wisdom he must seek
To look at Fool's Gold and not grow weak.

To capture a Crystal that is clear and pure.

To rescue Amethyst from the hollow.

His collection is growing as he
chooses what's right.
He tries his best each day and
prays each night.

Persistence pays off when he finds Calcite.

The end of his journey can now be seen.
The final stone remains, Aventurine.
To get it, he must receive favor from the Queen.

Now that Diamond Del has the jeweled crown,
He can either wear it...

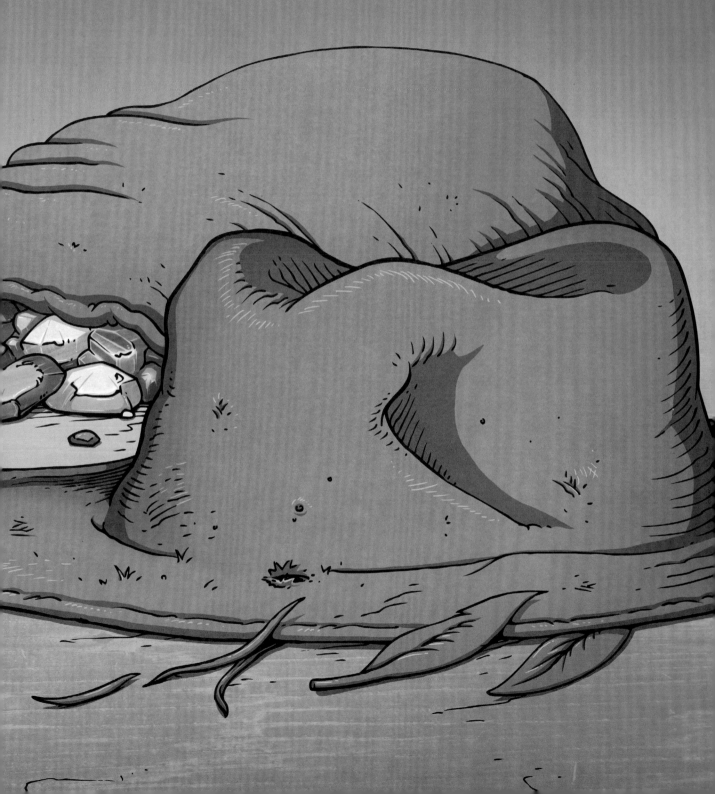

The King gladly held up the crown,
Revealing its beauty to the whole town.

"Diamond Del's treasures truly astound!
But what brings me pleasure
—is not just what he found—
But the virtues he displayed as he
journeyed around."

Definitions

Adventure: an undertaking usually involving danger and unknown risks

Courage: mental or moral strength to venture, persevere, and withstand danger, fear, or difficulty

Honor: a good name or public esteem based on merited respect

Peace: a state of tranquility, quiet, security, order, or harmony

Knowledge: the range of one's information or understanding

Wisdom: good sense, insight and judgment

Faith: firm belief in something for which there is no proof

Endure: to remain firm under suffering or misfortune without giving in

Integrity: firm adherence to a code of moral values

Loyalty: staying committed or devoted

Persistence: continuation without change for a longer than usual time

Favor: friendly regard shown toward another

Humble: not proud or arrogant, but modest and unassuming

Virtue: a standard of right living based on moral excellence

Diamond Del's Identification Chart

Fluorite is known as the most colorful mineral in the world. Its color range includes purple, blue, green, yellow, brown, pink, black, reddish orange, and colorless. It is a fluorescent mineral, which means it emits light under a UV lamp. It is used in making camera and telescope lenses, cooking utensils, and to manufacture steel. (Hardness 4)

Tiger Eye is a gem that contains tiny fibers that reflect light in an unusual way. When light reflects off it, it resembles light reflecting off a tiger or cat's eye. Tiger eye can be found in blue and red, but it most commonly appears in yellow. It is found mostly in Africa. (Hardness 7)

Rose Quartz is a pink colored quartz. The nickname for rose quartz is pink ice. The stone gets its pink coloring from the titanium impurities within it. Rose quartz is rarely found in the crystal formation common to the clear quartz. (Hardness 7)

Fool's Gold, also known as pyrite, is a shiny, yellow mineral that has a brassy look. Its nickname is "Fool's Gold" because it is often mistaken for gold. One way to tell the difference between the two is to hit it with a hammer. Pyrite will break into pieces while real gold will only bend. (Hardness 6)

Quartz is formed in many different shapes, colors, and sizes. Quartz is the most common mineral on Earth. Most of the sand on the beach is nothing more than tiny pieces of quartz. When quartz forms as a crystal, it will have a point and six sides if it has not been broken or crushed. The clearer the quartz, the more valuable it is. (Hardness 7)

Amethyst is a purple quartz crystal. It is the February birthstone and is one of the most popular stones worn in jewelry. It gets its purple color from iron impurities. Amethyst may be found in light to dark shades of purple. (Hardness 7)

Calcite is found in many different colors. One of the prettiest of these is orange. Calcite fizzles when it is placed in vinegar. Calcite is used to make chalk. (Hardness 3)

Aventurine is a green colored quartz. It comes in light to dark shades of green. Some shades of aventurine look a lot like emeralds, and it is often mistaken for emerald. And, just like an emerald, the aventurine can be polished into a beautiful green stone. (Hardness 7)